Young Bobby
El joven Bobby

Young Animal Pride Series
Serie: Jóvenes Animales Distinguidos

Book 10
Libro 10

Cataloging-in-Publication Data

Sargent, Dave, 1941–
    Young bobby = El joven bobby / by Dave
and Pat Sargent ; illustrated by Elaine Woodward.
—Prairie Grove, AR : Ozark Publishing, c2006.
        p. cm. (Young animal pride series ; 10)

    "Don't follow"—Cover.
    SUMMARY: Bobby tries to follow his
daddy but he can't swim. His daddy saves him.
        ISBN 1-59381-242-6 (hc)
                1-59381-243-4 (pbk)
                1-59381-244-2 (pfb)

    1. Bobcat—Juvenile fiction. [1. Bobcat—Fiction.
I. Sargent, Pat, 1936–   II. Woodward, Elaine, 1956– ill.
III. Title. IV. Series.

    PZ10.3.S243Bo 2006
    [Fic]—dc21   2003095974

Printed in the United States of America

Young Bobby
El joven Bobby

Young Animal Pride Series
Serie: Jóvenes Animales Distinguidos

Book 10   Libro 10

by Dave and Pat Sargent

Illustrated by Elaine Woodward

Ozark Publishing, Inc.
P. O. Box 228
Prairie Grove, AR 72753

Dave and Pat Sargent, authors of the extremely popular Animal Pride Series, visit schools all over the United States, free of charge. If you would like to have Dave and Pat visit your school, please ask your librarian to call 1-800-321-5671.

Foreword

When young Bobby meets his daddy, he really likes him. When Daddy Bobcat goes on a hunting trip, Bobby follows.

Prefacio

Al joven Bobby le gusta mucho estar con su papá. Cuando papá Lince sale de cacería, Bobby lo sigue.

My name is Bobby.

Mi nombre es Bobby.

I am a bobcat.

Soy un lince.

My fur is brown.

Mi pelaje es color café.

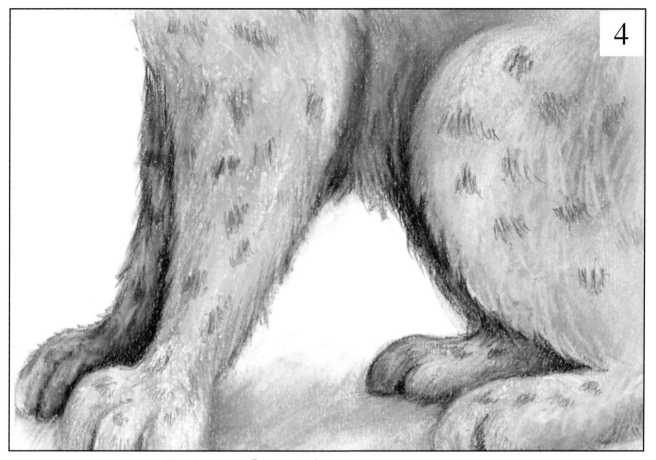

My fur has spots.

Mi pelaje tiene manchas.

I sleep all day.

Duermo todo el día.

I play at night.

Juego en la noche.

I live in a log.

Vivo en un tronco.

The log is hollow.

El tronco está hueco.

Look at my daddy.

Mira a mi papá.

My daddy is big.

Mi papá es grande.

Daddy went hunting.

Papá salió de cacería.

I followed him.

Lo seguí.

I tried to swim.

Traté de nadar.

Daddy heard me cry.

Papá me oyó llorar.

15

He jumped in.

Él saltó al agua.

He saved me.

Él me salvó.

My daddy purrs loud.

Mi papá ronronea muy fuerte.

Sometimes he caterwauls.

A veces maúlla.

I love my daddy.

Quiero a mi papá.